400

YOUNG MAN-OF-THE-HOUSE

YOUNG MAN OF THE HOUSE

By

MABEL LEIGH HUNT

Drawings by
LOUIS SLOBODKIN

A Stokes Book

J. B. LIPPINCOTT COMPANY

PHILADELPHIA AND NEW YORK

To STEVIE

CONTENTS

CONTENTS

ILLUSTRATIONS

YOUNG MAN-OF-THE-HOUSE

Father looked splendid in his new army uniform.

I

Captain Tuttle Goes to War

FATHER was going away. Eben and Jerry thought he looked splendid in his new army uniform. But strange—not quite like Father.

"In his gray suit he was a doctor," declared Jerry. "But in this suit he's a soldier."

"He is still a doctor," explained Eben. "He is going into the army to doctor the soldiers who get sick. So he has to dress like a soldier. It's a rule. One of Uncle Sam's rules."

Thoughtfully Jerry felt of Father's khaki trouser-leg. It did seem odd that even Uncle Sam should be able to boss such a knowing man as Father. But then he remembered. "Uncle Sam is not a real person," he said.

[3]

"Of course not," answered Eben.

"Of course not," echoed Jerry. A kid only five years old would know that. Jerry frowned. It was queer how you sometimes thought of Uncle Sam as real—a gentleman loved and respected by all, and whose name you often heard. Other times you thought of him as someone like Santa Claus. Or as a picture, or a red-white-and-blue costume in a play at school.

But it was really the fault of Great-grandfather Ebenezer, who hung in a large frame in Granzie's room at home, that Eben and Jerry had always felt rather mixed up in their minds about Uncle Sam. Because Great-grandfather Ebenezer, who had once been a real person, and Uncle Sam who is NOT a real person, looked so remarkably alike. It was their chin-whiskers that did it. As old as Eben was, there were still moments when he thought of

[4]

these two be-whiskered gentlemen at the same time.

Staring up at Father in his new army uniform made the boys' necks ache. For they were squeezed tight against him in the center of a close crowd of people. Mother and Granzie and baby Joe were there, too. Every member of the family, except Pansy. Father had said good-by to her at home.

Almost all the grown-ups in the village of Sidneyville had come to the little railroad station to see Father off. They milled about on the narrow platform, pushing forward to shake his hand and say good-by to him. Their talk and laughter were loud and hearty, to hide their regret at seeing him go. Jokes flew back and forth above the heads of Eben and Jerry like rubber balls they could not catch. The jokes made them feel small and forgotten. The crowd and the pushing made them feel small

[5]

and smothered. And what if they could not get out of this in time to have a good view of Number 29, the big, black locomotive, when it came roaring up to the station? They looked at each other, flushed and worried.

Father must have guessed. He must have known all along how uncomfortable they were. As neatly and quickly and firmly as only Father could, he now steered the boys out of the crowd, and down to the empty freight end of the station. Whee-oo, how wonderful to draw a good breath! To see something besides buttons and buckles and cuffs and thick bodies within an inch of one's nose! To look at the wide, frosty fields beyond the tracks, and to know they would be able to see Number 29 from the moment she thrust her nose around the bend.

Father hoisted the boys up on the baggage truck. He stood in front of them. His mouth was sober. But there were twinkles in his eyes, as always.

[6]

"What with being on the jump these past two weeks, paying final visits to my patients, closing my office, and turning over my practice to old Doctor Draper, I've had scarcely time to look at you boys. We've not even had time for any good old pillow-fights," said Father. He doubled up his fist, in fun, and aimed it at Jerry. Jerry dodged, but after all, Father's fist touched his middle as lightly as if it had been a toy balloon.

"Jerry-boy," said Father, "you are a big fellow of six. You can help your mother and Granzie—and me—simply by keeping out of mischief. You will be good, won't you, Son?"

Jerry nodded earnestly. He looked as good as an angel—a snub-nosed angel in brown corduroys.

"And you, Eben," said Father, laying a firm hand on Eben's shoulder, "you are nine. Quite old enough to have learned a thing or two. You will have to be man-of-the-house while I am gone.

[7]

Take good care of Mother and Granzie and Jerry and the baby and Pansy."

"All right, Father," promised Eben.

Father leaned over to kiss his sons. They hugged him tight, *tight*. Far away, beyond the bend, sounded the whistle of Number 29. Father gave each of the boys a playful little thump as they slid off the baggage truck. "I hope I shall not come back one of these days to hear my sons spoken of in Sidneyville as *those boys of Doctor Tuttle's.*" Even with the train clattering up to the station, and their hearts beating hard with excitement and a queer kind of pain, the way Father said "those boys" made Eben and Jerry blush.

There was a sudden flurry of last handshakes and shouts, hugs and kisses. The locomotive stopped, breathing with gentle puffs, waiting politely for Father. Before a fellow could quite believe it, there were Father's new brown army shoes

[8]

sturdily mounting the train steps. Then his face appeared at one of the coach windows, smiling at no one but Mother. A keen, honest American soldier's face, under a captain's cap.

"All abo-ward!" called the conductor, in a voice that sounded as if it came from a tunnel. "All abo-o-wa-ard!" echoed from far away across the fields. Number 29 gave a snort. She began working her sharp elbows. The conductor swung himself up to the step just in time. Eben had often wondered what would happen if ever the train should go off and leave the conductor standing on the platform? Would he be excited, and shout and bellow and run down the track after the train? Or would he be rather glad to spend a quiet little vacation in Sidneyville? Loaf in the ticket-office, and stroll about town, getting acquainted, and looking at all the houses? Maybe stay all night at the Sidneyville Hotel? Or at Judge Bailey's house,

[9]

which was the biggest. Or even at Doctor Tuttle's! Eben liked to think of that, and of the conductor sitting in their living-room 'in his blue uniform and cap, telling stories, and letting Eben and Jerry take turns at playing with his ticket punch.

But once more the conductor had safely made it. He had disappeared. The train was moving off. For a moment the boys raced alongside, waving and yelling at Father. Suddenly there were only the open tracks, and away in the distance, growing smaller and smaller, was the train and a feather of smoke.

Pansy the Third

THE family walked home from the station, because they were saving gas, as Uncle Sam had told everyone to do. Granzie kept up a cheerful stream of talk. In her arms baby Joe jabbered about the big train in a language all his own. The boys were quiet, because there was such a look on Mother's face. As if she weren't with them at all. To make sure, Eben and Jerry walked on either side of her, clinging tight to her hands. Oh, yes, it was very queer without Father. Not at all a pleasant feeling.

Still, there was one good thing about it. The boys didn't have to go to school until one o'clock, and that was three hours away. When they had changed their clothes from best to everyday, Jerry suggested they play "train."

"Okay," agreed Eben, "if you will let me be the locomotive." Playing "train" was a baby game. But all of Eben's friends were at school, and would not know. He would play it only to amuse little Jerry. Though it would be comforting just now to make a lot of noise.

"And I'll be Father, going away on the train," said Jerry.

Around the lawn and through the front and back porches Eben puffed and hissed and hooted. He made almost as much noise as old Number 29 herself. He chugged through the chicken yard and garden, working his elbows in furious imitation of moving piston-rods. Sometimes he drew to sudden halts, and his patient passenger would stumble against his heels. Sometimes he steamed slowly up imaginary mountains, and then tore down their

[12]

slopes, whirling around sharp curves and through the tunnel of the grape-arbor. And all the while Jerry was Father, a soldier-doctor going off to camp with a medical unit.

"But we ought to cross a railroad trestle," declared Eben, halting, red-faced and panting. "High!" He measured at shoulder level. The boys studied the landscape. There was nothing in sight that even faintly resembled a railroad trestle. Unless—Eben suddenly worked up steam, wheeled, and went puffing out through the front gate, along the sidewalk, and into the yard of Mr. Sawyer, the painter who lived next door. Jerry followed with perfect trust. Often these days a soldier had no idea where he was going.

Mr. Sawyer was a very special friend of Eben's. He didn't mind the boys coming over to play so long as they remembered that it was Mr. Sawyer's yard. Now it seemed as if he must have known

[13]

they were going to play "train." Though how could he? Anyway, he had left a pair of sawbucks standing very conveniently against his garage. Yonder was a long ladder, too. Just the thing!

"You take one end," commanded Eben. Moving and spacing the sawbucks was easy. "They're as light as feathers," scoffed Eben.

But placing the ladder across them took some tugging and heaving. "It's exactly like a railroad trestle, now," crowed Jerry, in triumph. He stood off to admire it until he saw that Locomotive Eben was backing up. Eben took position at the street end of Mr. Sawyer's driveway. Puffing out his cheeks, he shuffled off, with Jerry close behind. When they reached the sawbuck, Eben scrambled to its top, and after a moment's pause, sped nimbly across the ladder.

But it was a bit of a struggle for little Jerry to mount the sawbuck. And the spaces between the

He was face down on the driveway, howling.

rungs of the ladder were wide for his short legs. As he began to take each careful little jump, Eben reached the other sawbuck. He sprang upon the free end of the poorly-balanced ladder. Down it went, like a teeter-totter. Up went the other end, and Jerry with it. Eben leaped to safety just before the ladder did a heavy flop and clattered to the ground. But the trusting traveler—where was he? Poor Jerry, he was face down on the driveway, howling.

"What's all this rumpus?" cried Mrs. Sawyer, rushing from her house like a hen with spread wings. She picked Jerry up. She led him home. Eben followed meekly. He had to explain to Mother about the railway wreck.

Above Jerry's plasters, Mother looked sadly at Eben. "Too bad," she said, "and your father scarcely out of sight. One of the last things he

[17]

told me was of your promise to be man-of-the-house."

"I'm sure Eben didn't tip the ladder on purpose," said Granzie, hastily. "He is only a boy."

This seemed all too true. Eben went to school without Jerry, who had a thumping headache as a result of the train wreck. Eben was sorry. On the way home from school, he bought a sucker for Jerry with his very own money. And in memory of Father, who was by this time no-one-knew-how-far-away, Eben bought a cabbage for Pansy. Pansy loved cabbage. And Father loved Pansy.

Because Father was a doctor, he belonged to the American Medical Association, and the State Medical Society. But on account of Pansy, he also belonged to the American Jersey Cattle Club. For Pansy was that kind of a cow—a Jersey. "The best," Father always declared. "The kind my dad had when I was a boy on the farm. A Jersey has

[18]

everything," Father would say. "Beauty, a gentle disposition, and the richest, yellowest milk. Yes, siree, a Jersey for me, ten times out of ten."

Everybody but the Tuttles, and the Sawyers next door, and Mrs. Hill down the street, who also used Pansy's milk, and paid for it, had bottles left on their doorsteps by the dairyman who drove out daily from Edenburn. Pansy was the only cow in Sidneyville. You couldn't really count Butterball Wicker, because she lived outside the town limits, beyond the baseball diamond that was called Wicker's Field. Even if Butterball had lived in town, you could have scarcely counted her. Because she was so far below Pansy in the social scale.

Pansy was high-born. She had a pedigree. It was printed in fancy lettering. It hung in Father's study in a black-and-gold frame. Father was proud of it. He always showed it to callers who had never seen it before. Sometimes he forgot and showed

[19]

it to the same people more than once. Pansy herself might have been snooty about her pedigree if she had known about it. For it proved beyond a doubt that Pansy was of noble birth. It listed the names of all her grannies and all her grandsires. For ten generations back! There was not a rascal nor a hussy among them. They were all aristocrats.

The grannies had lovely names. Golden Lady and Golden Cloud, for instance. Aurora and Phyllis and Dawn Queen. Father said that Aurora had been the most famous of them all. She had lived to the ripe old age of thirty-six, and had had twenty-five children. And because there had been two Pansy's before Pansy Tuttle, she was called Pansy the Third on the pedigree.

As for Pansy's grandfathers—what magnificent fellows they must have been! You could almost hear them bellow when you read their names:

[20]

Trumpeter, Stampede, Village Beau, Island Ruler, Silver Comet.

Some of Father's friends razzed him about keeping a cow in town, and about his pride in Pansy herself. Once Pansy was ailing. Father was worried. So Fred Goff, the druggist with whom Father sometimes went fishing, sent Pansy a huge bouquet of dahlias. It was tied with wide purple ribbon. There was a get-well card tucked among the flowers. The druggist had selected it from his stock in the store. The card said:

> *Just a bright and gay "Hello"*
> *To cheer you, and to let you know*
> *How very, very glad I'll be*
> *To hear of your Recovery.*
>
> "Love from Fred Goff."

Father just roared. Because by that time Pansy was much better, anyway.

[21]

There was a Pansy the Third account book in Father's desk. On the left-hand pages, under the word "Expenditures" Father would write the sums he spent for feed and pasture. Also what he paid Roy the handy man for cleaning her stable and doing the morning milking.

The right-hand pages in the account book were headed with the word "Profits." Under this Father would proudly write the number of gallons of milk Pansy gave, the pounds of butter that were made from her rich, yellow cream, and the sales to the Sawyers and to Mrs. Hill. At the end of the year the total sounded very impressive, and Father would tell everyone in town.

But he never seemed to notice that the figures under "Expenditures" were very much larger than those under "Profits." He would point to his family and grin and say, "See my nice plump family? That's Pansy's doings." They were all

[22]

plump except Eben and Father himself. "It's natural for Eben and me to be thin," said Father, excusing Pansy from all responsibility.

Besides the fancy price Father had paid for his fine Jersey cow in the first place, he had hired Mr. Sawyer to build a neat house for her. Father had fitted it up in a style worthy of Pansy and her noble ancestry. Electric lights and everything. The best of food, such as soybean oil meal and cottonseed meal from the feed store. And a beautiful pale crystal of salt for Pansy to lick. In summer Father was always coming home from the country with the back end of his car full of green alfalfa hay and red clover and corn and carrots. He liked to stand with his foot on a fence rail and a piece of straw in his mouth and talk to some farmer about cows. But particularly of Pansy. They would sometimes discuss chickens, too. Because Father had a flock of White Wyandottes. But everyone

[23]

thought of the Wyandottes as belonging to Granzie. Partly because she looked after them, and
partly because they played second fiddle to Pansy,
in Father's affections.

Mother never complained about the money
Father spent on Pansy. She never laughed at him.
"It's on account of his fond boyhood memories,
bless him," she explained. "And it's good for a
busy doctor to have a hobby such as Pansy." And
every month, when the *Cow and Hen Journal*
came in the mail, Mother smoothed it out flat, and
laid it down, very gently, on the table by Father's
big easy chair, along with his medical journals and
other magazines. Father always read the *Cow and
Hen Journal* from cover to cover.

Before Father left for the army he said, "Perhaps we had better sell Pansy." He said it in a very
low voice, as if he didn't mean it. As if he were
afraid that Mother might agree. How happy he

[24]

was when Granzie and Mother cried out, "Sell Pansy? Surely you don't mean it! Why, it would be like selling baby Joe!"

Father had taught Eben to milk. Eben always did the evening milking, except when something was going on that was very important, and he couldn't get home in time. Then Granzie did it, or Roy, who was Sidneyville's handiest handy man.

So this evening, when Eben carried the cabbage to Pansy, he patted her. He scratched her between her horns. He even took down the brush and gave her a few strokes, though Roy curried her every morning. And he did the milking so well that one might have thought him a master dairyman. "Take good care of Pansy," Father had said. To look after Pansy the Third, the pedigreed cow that was Father's hobby—that would be a great responsibility. It would be a part of the whole business of being man-of-the-house.

PANSY THE THIRD

III

Conversation at Night

AFTER the milking was done, Eben made sure that the gate to the cow-lot was fastened—the one leading into the alley. He went in to supper. What a queer feeling Father's empty chair gave him! He thought about suggesting to Mother that he might occupy it, so it wouldn't look so lonely. But of course that wouldn't do. Nobody could take Father's place.

After supper Eben dried the dishes for Granzie, while Mother put the baby to bed. As she was writing her first letter to Father, Eben read a story to Jerry, and then he did his homework. Without the least urging. He won a shining smile from

Mother. "Let's see now," he thought, all warmed up inside, "what does a man-of-the-house do before his family goes to bed? Oh, yes, I know."

Eben then went about briskly, locking the doors with flourishes and testing the windows. Father always said it was foolish to lock up, in such a well-behaved little place as Sidneyville. But he did it every night, because to Granzie Sidneyville was quite a town, and she couldn't sleep, she said, with the doors unlocked.

There was the Seth Thomas clock to wind, too, thought Eben, remembering more and more manly duties. While Mother was finishing her letter in the library, and Granzie was in the kitchen taking her nightly dose of soda-water, Eben mounted a slender-legged chair. He opened the door of the clock on the mantel. Between thumb and forefinger he drew out the key, carefully, so

[27]

as not to disturb the swing of the pendulum, just as he had often seen Father do. The spring grew tight as Eben turned the key.

Ouch! He felt a sudden sharp cramp in his thumb. He couldn't help hopping with pain. The fragile chair wobbled. Eben clawed the air. There was a tinkle of glass, and on the hearth lay the ruins of the blue glass hat that had stood on the mantel ever since Eben could remember.

Mother and Granzie came rushing in. "Oh-h-h!" breathed Mother. "My dear Aunt Minna gave that little hat to me when I was only five!" It was as if Mother were bidding good-by forever to a precious bit of her childhood.

"Do you know, I always expected the doctor to brush the glass hat off the mantel, too, when *he* wound the clock," declared Granzie.

In the night, perhaps because of the railroad wreck and the sad thing that had happened to the

[28]

glass hat, Eben wakened. He heard the whistle of the ten-forty express, its thundering flight through the outskirts of Sidneyville, and again its deep, long-drawn wail echoing through the dark, silent countryside. A chill ran up Eben's spine and crawled coldly into his scalp. He got up and tiptoed into Mother's room. She was awake, too. "What is it, Son?" she asked, quietly.

"I'm lonesome," said Eben, standing forlorn and skinny by Mother's bed.

"Why did Father leave us?" he whispered, presently, from the place that Mother made for him in her bed.

Mother smoothed his hair. She was silent for a moment. Then she said, "War is cruel and dreadful, Eben. It is the wrong way of settling arguments. All sensible folk know that. But sometimes certain wicked ones set themselves up as leaders and start wars before we are scarcely aware of the

[29]

danger. All of a sudden they are showering us with their bombs and bullets, before we have had a chance to say to them, 'Why can't we arrange this? Won't you agree to that?'

"So now we find ourselves in this greatest war of all. And although war itself is wrong indeed, behind it, for us, are the things that are completely right—the great and noble ideals we cherish and must always keep—the sense of justice and humanity that makes us fly to the rescue of downtrodden peoples. It is strange and wonderful and beautiful, Eben, how danger calls forth hidden greatness. Every man wants to share that danger. He wants to give whatever strength and skill and bravery he has to give. He wants to feel that he has a share in the great events that are shaping the world. That is why your father, and men like him, have gone forth to war, much as they love their families and the comfort and safety of their homes.

[30]

"But you and Jerry, Son, and other boys every-where, will owe a great debt to our brave fighters of today. You can pay it by growing into wiser men than the world has ever known. Men so wise and just, so understanding of all peoples that you will be able to settle trouble and trouble-makers without dreadful bullets and bombs. Without kill-ing, Eben."

Mother made Father's going, and the war, easier to understand. And how safe and comfortable he felt here, by her side! He had meant to tell her how sorry he was about the glass hat, and not tak-ing better care of Jerry. How he truly meant to be—well, scarcely a real man-of-the-house like Father, but at least a *young* man-of-the-house. But that seemed very small beside the big, brave things Mother had been talking about. And before he could have said it, he had fallen fast asleep.

IV

The Polka-Dotted Necktie

EVERY day Mother wrote a letter to Father. And almost every day there came a letter from Father addressed to Mrs. John Tuttle. That was Mother. Father's letters made the days so much happier. He always sent a special message to Granzie, and one to Eben and one to Jerry. Father even sent messages to baby Joe, which he was too young to understand, but so funny they made everyone laugh.

Once there came a letter addressed to Pansy the Third.

"Dear Pansy," wrote Father. "Will you stop chewing your cud long enough to listen to this?

Or can you read it yourself? I never thought to ask you that before. No doubt your grandsire *Island Ruler* could read. Anyone with a name like that! If you have been keeping anything from me, Pansy, and can really read, I would strongly recommend to you the *Cow and Hen Journal*. Reading of what other cows are doing in the world, or even hens, would, no doubt, inspire you to greater accomplishments. But you are okay, Pansy. Although I have not seen many cows since I joined the army, I am sure there is none other I would like half so well, nor who is so beautiful as you. It is patriots like you, on the Home Front, who are working hard to furnish the world with food. I am glad to hear that your friend Eben Tuttle is taking good care of you. Tell him and Master Jerry that I shall write a special letter to them very soon. With love and best wishes,

Captain John Tuttle."

[33]

Eben and Jerry simply rolled on the floor when Mother read this aloud. Especially at the picture Father drew on the margin of his letter, showing Pansy, with spec's on, reading the *Cow and Hen Journal*. They carried the letter out to her stable and read it to her. She turned her large, soft gaze upon them, but she went right on chewing her cud.

"What is cud?" asked Jerry, when they had stopped laughing again.

Eben thought a moment. He liked to be able to answer Jerry's questions, since he was older and had learned a thing or two. Now it was more important than ever, since Father was not here to give the right answer, always.

"Cud is something like chewing-gum. I think," he added, cautiously.

Jerry walked around and squatted down in front of Pansy, trying to see into her mouth. What a huge piece of chewing-gum she must be working

They read the letter to Pansy.

on! "I can't see it," he announced. "Where does she get it?"

"Not at the drugstore," answered Eben. "She keeps it in her stomach, and brings it up into her mouth, somehow, the way cows do, whenever she wants to chew again."

Jerry thought this would be convenient, but it didn't sound very attractive. He made a wry little face. "And does she keep it in a back tooth and save it when she is eating hay, and things?"

"I s'pose," answered Eben. "Father would know." He changed the subject, quickly. "I wonder when Father's letter will come to us."

"Tomorrow," said Jerry. He was sure of it. When he came home from school at noon the next day he was astonished to hear that the letter had not come. A letter to Mother, but none to Jerry and Eben. On the way back to school he stopped at the post-office. He thumped on the shelf below

the wicket. The postmaster could just see the top
of his head and his round brown eyes.

"Any letter for Jerry and Eben Tuttle?" piped
Jerry.

The postmaster took a step and glanced into the
other side of the Tuttle lock-box. "Nope," he said.
"And I remember now. Your grandmother got all
the mail this morning. Sidneyville has but one
mail a day, youngster."

"Somepin might of been lost," insisted Jerry.
"Look on the floor."

"I wasn't made the postmaster of Sidneyville to
go dropping United States mail helter-skelter on
the floor, young man," said the postmaster. "Now
run along."

Jerry walked meekly out of the post-office. But
he didn't believe the postmaster. Father had said
"very soon." Today was "soon." Very. So of course
the letter was there. In the afternoon he stopped

in again. By this time the postmaster would have found it, lying on the floor, or mixed up with some other letters or even in the bottom of the mail-bag. But the post-office was empty and quiet. The wickets were closed. Jerry thumped again, and waited. "Hey," he called faintly. But no one came. Suddenly Jerry felt the strongest dislike for the postmaster.

But he forgot it the next day, which was Saturday. Because there was the letter! It was addressed to Master Jerry Tuttle and Master Ebenezer Tuttle. For a fleeting moment Eben didn't know who Master Ebenezer Tuttle could be. But of course it was Eben himself, named for Great-grandfather Ebenezer, in the frame in Granzie's room.

Jerry said that he should be the one to open the envelope, because his name came first. Eben said he was the oldest, so of course he should open it. They had a little scuffle over it, until Granzie

[39]

rescued it, all crumpled. She smoothed it out, and read it aloud. It was very interesting. It told the boys all about Father's first ride in a big plane. How he felt, to be way up in the sky. How the fields and towns looked, and a little about the inside workings of the plane.

It was wonderful to think of Father actually riding in an airplane. Almost too wonderful to believe. Eben's spirits seemed suddenly too big for his body. He wanted to fly, too. Or climb a lofty steeple, or do some high jumping. At least, something intensely airy.

The house in which the Tuttles lived was a tall, old-fashioned one. When the boys stood in the lower front hall, they could look up and see where the stair rail spiraled to its last whorl on the third floor. It had always been fun to slide down the long, winding balusters. Within fifteen minutes after reading of Father's ride in a plane, Eben and Jerry had two or three slides.

But today such sport did not seem nearly daring enough. From the garage Eben brought a long coil of rope. He climbed the two flights of stairs. Jerry followed. He watched while Eben tied one end of the rope to the loftiest curve of the baluster. Its length was flung into space. The boys peered over to see it dangling into the lower hall.

"Look!" said Eben. He climbed over the rail, grasped the rope with both hands, and let himself down, inch by inch. Then he gave himself a push against the stairs with his foot. He began swinging back and forth. What fun, bumping now against the stairway, now against the upper wall! And to feel himself so high above the hall rug on the first floor!

"Watch me make a power dive!" he called to

[41]

Jerry. "Whee-ee-ee!" He skimmed down the rope and landed far below.

"Hey!" cried Jerry, in delight. "I'm going to make a power dive, too."

"No, Jerry! Wait! It's not what you think it is!" He plodded up the two flights, and held out his hands. Jerry stared. Eben's palms were already puffy with blisters. In places the skin was chafed raw and red. "Gee, but they hurt!" said Eben, blowing on them. Gingerly he untied the rope and dragged it off downstairs before Jerry could take a power dive, in spite of warnings.

Mother swabbed Eben's burns with moistened soda. "That was very dangerous," she said. "Especially if little Jerry had tried it. I thought you knew better, Ebenezer Tuttle. How grieved Father would be if he knew you are not always man-of-the-house!"

"The lad didn't cry over his poor hands," reminded Granzie.

"Watch me make a power dive!" he called to Jerry.

"I could be man-of-the-house, maybe," mur-mured Eben, half to himself, "if I could only re-member to be."

He must think of something that would help him remember. Father was the finest man in the world, and Mother the nicest woman. Granzie was the most wonderful grandmother. He did want to please them all, and to keep his promise to Father.

One day he came home from school to find his mother sorting over Father's clothing, the civilian clothes he had worn before joining the army. Mother was sending some of the suits and sweaters to the cleaner. Others were being brushed and sprayed and hung away in clean muslin bags. At this particular moment Mother was looking over Father's neckties. She placed certain ones in a box between layers of tissue paper. Others she dropped in a little pile on the floor by her chair.

Eben looked at Mother. Surely she was not

going to throw away anything that belonged to
Father. As if she guessed what was in his thoughts,
she said, "Some of these ties are worn, Eben. And
some are downright disgraceful. Granzie is going
to clean them and cut them into strips and crochet
them into a round mat for her bedside table. So
you see they won't be thrown away, after all."
Mother smiled. Her voice was tender and a little
shaky. "Dear funny daddy, it was never safe to let
him select his own ties. He chose such terrible ones
without ever dreaming they weren't quite all
right."

Eben picked up one of the ties that Mother
would not keep for Father because she said it was
terrible. It was a sickly green, with liver-colored
polka dots. Eben couldn't see anything the matter
with it. In fact, he thought it was handsome, and
as new as if it had never been worn. And indeed
it had not, owing to Mother's poor opinion of it.

Eben rolled the tie carefully, and slipped it into his pocket. Granzie wouldn't mind. There were plenty of others left for her table-mat. But when he appeared at the supper table that evening, Mother and Granzie cried out in high-pitched duet. "Whatever in the world?"

"It's to remind me to be man-of-the-house," explained Eben, calmly buttering his bread. Around his neck was one of Father's old collars, much too large, but tied together with a bit of string. The disgraceful tie, which also helped to anchor the collar, dangled over Eben's chest.

Mother looked at Granzie. There was a tiny pucker of worry on her forehead. "He must be like his father, when it comes to ties," she said.

Granzie chuckled. When the dessert was brought in, she told Eben he might have her share.

Eben wore the tie to school the next morning, around the neck of his pull-over. "Oh, dear," murmured Mother, gazing after him. "It seems to mean so much to Eben. But what will his teacher think of me, allowing him to go to school looking like that?"

"Let him be," laughed Granzie. "I rather think he is wearing that tie the same as a knight of old wore his knot of ribbon—to help him to victory."

Eben's teacher pretended not to notice the necktie. Neither did it create much stir among the children. Florabelle Marshall and her chum, Marylou, giggled, but Eben didn't care. Girls often giggled over nothing. And on the playground at recess something so interesting happened that even Eben forgot the tie. Or almost.

It seemed that Beany McBean had something to tell the other boys. They went into a huddle. "See, fellas?" whispered Beany. "From now on let's call Owen Bradley 'Peaches.' 'Cause this is what his aunt said to the Methodist minister's wife th'other day." Beany raised his voice to a mouse-like squeak. "Don't you think my little nephew Owen Bradley is a dear? His complexion is just like peaches-and-cream," cooed Beany, in mimicry of the fond aunt.

The boys straightened up, their faces glistening with glee. They stood off from the Bradley boy, four against one. "Hi, Peaches!" taunted Chuckie Howard.

Young Bradley's face flushed from pink to red, and paled from red to white. But he answered, quick as a wink. "Hi, Tomato!" That was because of Chuckie's red hair.

Now it was Tommy Eaton's turn. "Hi, Peaches!" said Tommy from above folded arms.

"Hi, Punkin!" answered Peaches. *"Elephant!"* he added, looking fat Tommy over with chill scorn.

[49]

Eben now took a step forward. "Peaches!" he hissed.

"Poker Dot!" hissed Peaches. That would be because of the necktie with the liver-colored polka-dots. It was secretly fascinating to the boys to hear the ready and extremely fitting answers to their taunts. Peaches was smart. No wonder, a guy who read so many books!

"Hi, Peaches," yelled Beany. "Peaches—and cream!"

"I wouldn't talk if I were you," sneered Peaches. "You're nothing but a bean." Which was almost true, since Beany's name was McBean. Edgar Mc-Bean, son of the florist, E. McBean. Peaches went on. "Your father's a bean. Your grandfather is a bean. Your great-grandfather was a bean. Your great-great—"

This was more than Beany could take. He and Peaches were about to square off, when the janitor strolled up, took hold of them, and said, "Hi, you!" Just then the gong sounded.

So that was that! And Owen Bradley had a new nickname that suited him to a T. When the boys marched into the schoolhouse, Miss Jennings, the principal, drew Eben out of line. She took him into her office. Eben thought it must have something to do with Peaches. But Miss Jennings said, "Now! What about this—this thing around your neck?"

She listened kindly when Eben said, "It's my father's tie, and he's gone away." That was enough to say. For of course a fellow doesn't tell just anyone the things that are sort of secret things inside of him.

Miss Jennings said, brightly, "Oh, yes, I understand. The Home Front."

Eben didn't see what his father's necktie had to do with the Home Front, unless Miss Jennings

[51]

was trying to be funny and meant that a man always wears his tie at the front of his neck. But one does not argue with principals. And before he left Miss Jennings' office, Eben had agreed not to wear the over-sized collar and tie to school any more. In fact, with Miss Jennings' help, he took it off then and there. The principal said, "We like our boys and girls to appear as neat as possible, in clothing suitable to their years. Clothing that won't start any foolish fads, or revolutions either, in the school," she added.

But Eben had already decided that Miss Jennings liked the same kind of neckties that Mother liked, and not the ones he and Father thought were handsome.

When Jerry saw how seriously Eben wore Father's collar-and-tie, he wanted one.

"It was me Father told to be man-of-the-house," objected Eben. "He only told you to be good."

They were beginning to argue, when Granzie said, "I can't spare any more ties, Jerry dear, if my crochet work is to be a success. So that settles it."

Mother wrote to Father. "Eben's neckwear gives me the shudders. The tie is even worse than when you bought it, my dear. But its effect on Eben is rather surprising. He is quite the young man-of-the-house."

Eben did not know what Mother had said, of course. But Granzie smiled at him proudly and said, "Eben is like my side of the family. It beats all how much he resembles his great-grandfather Ebenezer."

V

Mr. Sawyer, Next-Door Neighbor

So EBEN continued to wear Father's collar-and-tie in the privacy of home, whenever he remembered it. Sometimes he wore it when he called for a chat with his friend Mr. Sawyer, who lived next door. Mr. Sawyer never wore a tie except on Sundays, and then a neat black bow. But he gazed at Eben's neckwear with real admiration.

"As handsome a tie as ever I saw," he declared. "Reminds me of your dad, somehow. Green's always a good color. Sensible, yet lively. Like grass and trees an' things. And I s'pose you've noticed, like as not, that spring is on its way." There was an odd little lilt in Mr. Sawyer's voice.

"You'll be painting your house, then, won't you?" asked Eben.

"Soon as I can sneak some time away from painting other folkses houses. Mostly on Saturdays it will be."

How Mr. Sawyer said "Saturdays!" In such a gay and tender way. Because Mr. Sawyer simply adored making houses bright and clean with fresh paint. But especially his own house. He would have painted it each spring, but Mrs. Sawyer said, firmly, "Every three years is often enough."

So Eben knew that was why Mr. Sawyer could scarcely wait for spring. Because this was the year to paint again.

"Saturdays?" asked Eben. "Then maybe you'd like me to help you," he offered.

"As a matter of fact, I might," answered Mr. Sawyer. "It's a funny thing, though. Anybody under fifteen that tries to do a serious painting job is mighty liable to get painters' colic."

"Did you ever have it?" asked Eben, looking hard at Mr. Sawyer.

"No, but I didn't take up painting till I was nineteen. Now I'm so old and tough, likely I'll never have painter's colic. Leastways I hope not. But take you—so young and tender, why, dog-bite-it, you'd double up in no time. But I'd be pleased to have you help me decide on the color to paint my house."

So, whenever there was time, Eben and Mr. Sawyer might be seen bending over color charts, and studying advertisements that Mr. Sawyer had saved. He had a stack of them, pictures of perfectly charming houses, all speckless and dazzling in new paint. Gravely Eben and Mr. Sawyer discussed the various combinations.

"This is pretty," Eben would say. "Buff, with

"Whadda you think of dove-gray with slate-colored trim?"

tile-red for the scroll-work and the window-shutters."

"Yeah," agreed Mr. Sawyer. "But a mite new-fangled. When it comes to paint, a painter has to keep his head and not go making a fool of himself, setting an outlandish style for others to copy. Therefore," said Mr. Sawyer, peering wisely over his glasses at Eben, "a painter's own house has got to be the very pink of perfection. Elegant, yet modest. Whadda you think of dove-gray, with slate-colored trim?"

"Nothing to it," declared Eben. "Now how about painting your house the same colors as this necktie, maybe?"

That would be, of course, dull green, with liver-colored polka-dots. No, liver-colored *trim*.

Mrs. Sawyer just sat and rocked while Eben and Mr. Sawyer threshed out the question of colors. She never said a word, not even when they finally decided on white, with green trim. Eben thought it was very nice of her to leave it all to the men-folk. But of course Mrs. Sawyer knew beforehand that Mr. Sawyer would paint the house white-and-green. Because that was what he had painted it three years ago. And the time before that he had painted it white-and-green. And even the time before that! One might almost say that Mr. Sawyer's house has been *born* white-and-green.

It took Mr. Sawyer many Saturdays to paint his house, because he had a host of other jobs, both in Sidneyville and in Edenburn, the county seat ten miles away. He was at the top of his tallest scaffold one morning when Eben came over to talk. It was early in April. Sidneyville's fruit trees were a froth of airy blossom, and Mr. Sawyer had a good view of them. He whistled softly.

But he stopped when Eben hove into sight. In

spite of being so far away, he was as chummy as possible. He peered over his brush at Eben. "You look different," he said. "It's your tie. Or rather, it ain't your tie."

"The tie's gone," answered Eben, sadly. "I can't find it anywhere. I s'pose you've noticed me not wearing the collar lately. It kept getting kind of dirty. Granzie washed it for me, but Mother said it had better go into the furnace. I didn't mind so much. It was the necktie that really mattered." Eben fell silent, watching Mr. Sawyer slapping paint on the gable, right under the highest peak.

"Mr. Sawyer," he called, presently, "how about you and me building an airplane? We could take people up in it for rides and make a lot of money."

Mr. Sawyer edged along the scaffold. He was slow about answering, but Eben was used to that. "Well, I dunno," said the painter, at last. "It would take gas to fly it, a sight of it. And we're not supposed to be taking pleasure jaunts these days. Gas is for our bombers."

"Oh," answered Eben. Such a ninny he was for not remembering that!

"Why d'you want to make so much money?" asked Mr. Sawyer, kindly. "I'd say you were pretty well off, with that forty cents your mother pays you every week for looking after Pansy and milking her."

"You see, at school we are buying war stamps," explained Eben. "Great-grandfather Eb—I mean, Uncle Sam wants us to."

"Sure," agreed Mr. Sawyer.

"It's slow as molasses, buying stamps when a fellow makes only forty cents a week. What with other things to buy. That's why I've got to earn more."

"I don't blame you," said Mr. Sawyer. "Just

[62]

give me time. It's surprising how many things a fellow can study on while he paints. So maybe I can figure out a way you can earn."

"Okay," answered Eben. "Be sure and think of some BIG way, Mr. Sawyer."

VI

Saturday Baseball, and a Baby

IT RAINED for almost three weeks. When people
met each other on the cold, wet, windy streets they
shook their heads, gloomily. "We shall have no
fruit this summer," they would complain. "How
shall we ever get our gardens planted?" And Mr.
Sawyer could not do any outside painting, either.

Granzie caught a touch of the flu. Old Doctor
Draper said she must remain in bed for a few days.
It was hard for Granzie to "stay put," as she ex-
pressed it. Especially when a Saturday came that
was crystal clear and almost as warm as summer.
Perhaps the tiresome rains were over. Spades and
rakes were hauled out. The wet earth in Sidneyville gardens was turned over to dry, so that some

[64]

planting could be done the first thing next week. Roy, the handy man, worked in the Tuttle garden. Mr. Sawyer said he thought he could finish the white painting on his house that morning. "This afternoon I'll mix my green," he said, happily.

And when Eben went to the drugstore on an errand for Granzie, he overheard Fred Goff, the druggist, say that the Sidneyville High School baseball team would get out for a little practice. "At last," said the druggist.

Eben fairly pranced home. The year before he had sometimes been allowed to serve as bat-boy for the team. He would restore the bats to the basket, run after foul balls, and carry drinking water to the players. Besides feeling very useful and important on the field, Eben had a good opportunity to study the game. For he was a ballplayer himself. He belonged to the little boys' team that called itself the Bearcats. Oh, this was a glori-

[65]

ous day, and except for Father's being gone, Eben felt as happy as the happiest of robins.

But for Jerry it was not a glorious day. He had the toothache. Mother telephoned the dentist in Edenburn, while Jerry listened, glumly nursing his cheek. When Mother hung up the receiver, she said, "The dentist will see us at a quarter to two this afternoon."

"Going to take Joe with you?" asked Eben. "Of course?" He tried to be off-hand about it, but his voice squeaked with anxiety. For Mother was gazing at him with a certain look in her eye. Was this wonderful day to be utterly ruined?

"I can't very well look after both Jerry and Joe, without Granzie," answered Mother. "I don't want her even to know that I'm going away. She would be sure to get up and dress. Dear, you will have to take care of the baby. I shall hurry back from Edenburn just as soon as I can."

[66]

"Heck!" exclaimed Eben. His voice rose to a wail. "Mother! Today? Why, Mother, I've got to go to an important ball game. They'll be expecting me. I can't let them down. D'you want me to be like that—a guy like that?"

"Sh-h-h!" warned Mother. "I'm so sorry, Eben. Especially on the first fine Saturday we've had. I know how you feel, dear, but of course there are other boys in town who can do errands for the team." Mother smiled at him.

Eben looked sternly back at her. This was no time for smiles. "Maybe Mrs. Sawyer would keep Joe," he suggested. "Want me to run and ask her?"

"She told me she was going to get at her house-cleaning today, Saturday or not," answered Mother. "Of course I couldn't ask her to keep Joey."

"I'll bet Roy's wife would come, then," said Eben.

"She works at the bakery every Saturday," said Mother. "Saturday is a busy time for everyone. Eben, think how many soldiers there are today who would rather be playing ball, or sitting on the bleachers in their home towns! Instead of being far, far away, doing the hard things they are doing! Father, too." Mother's lips closed, sternly, in a way that Eben had learned to understand. It meant that the subject was closed.

Baby Joe wakened from his nap that afternoon a few minutes after Mother and Jerry had taken the bus for Edenburn. It was a delightful surprise to find himself hauled out of bed by his big brother. He was perfectly happy while Eben stuffed him awkwardly into his overalls and little sweater. When Eben muttered "Heck," and "Cripes," and "Dog-bite-it," borrowed from Mr. Sawyer, why, Joe thought they were words of endearment! He smiled his broadest smiles. When

"Dog-bite-it!" muttered Eben.

At that, Granzie went into her room. She came back at once. "If that's all that ails you," she said, "here is one tie I decided not to use in my little table rug. Though land knows it's gaudy enough. You may have it."

The tie was beautiful. Pale orange, with dizzy curlicues in black. Eben looped it around his neck.

Suddenly he scrambled out of bed, and began pulling on his clothes. "The milking!" he cried. "Mother forgot, when she sent me to bed, that I'm the milker around here!" Eben flashed past Granzie and down the back stairs pell-mell. The tie flew like a banner.

"Well, I declare!" said Granzie to herself. "Such a mixed-up boy! Careless as can be one moment, and the next, remembering his duty." Granzie chuckled as she straightened Eben's tumbled bed. "I'm beginning to believe there's some good magic in the doctor's neckties, myself!"

But Mother and Eben had a talk that evening. "Do you think you ought to be allowed to go to Wicker's Field next Saturday?" asked Mother.

Eben nodded. Then he shook his head.

"I was sure you would agree that you should not," said Mother. "After that, it will depend. And a father's necktie can never take the place of a boy's own thoughtfulness and sense of responsibility. Do you think a soldier performs his hard duty only because he wears a uniform?"

Eben nodded. Then he shook his head. Sometimes, when grown-ups ask you questions, suddenly, before you have had time to think them out yourself, it is not always clear whether they expect you to nod your head, or to shake it.

"But will Joey have the painter's colic, Mother?" asked Eben.

"Of course not," said Mother. "Where did you ever hear of a disease like that?"

[88]

VIII

The Rug That Crawled

IT WOULD be embarrassing, thought Eben, to meet Mr. Sawyer. After what had happened. But the painter never once mentioned unpleasant things, such as spilled green paint, or runaway babies. Or runaway boys, for that matter. Mr. Sawyer was just as kind and friendly as ever.

"That's a niftier tie, if anything, than the other one," said Mr. Sawyer. For in spite of what Mother had said, Eben was wearing the necktie that Granzie had given him. He felt sure that a tie of Father's had a very good influence on his behavior.

"And I've been thinking," said Mr. Sawyer, "how you could make some money to buy war stamps. I can't seem to settle on any one way for a boy of your age, but—"

"Nothing BIG?" cried Eben. For a moment he felt that Mr. Sawyer had failed him.

"There's hardly any of us makes BIG money in a BIG way," answered Mr. Sawyer. "Most of us do right well just plodding along steady. Working, and saving. And liking it, too. But if you keep your eyes open, and look sharp, I fancy you can find several little odd jobs around this here town."

"Uh-hunh," answered Eben, half-heartedly. Surely during all those hours of painting, Mr. Sawyer might have thought of some exciting adventure into big business.

Still, Eben had learned that Mr. Sawyer generally knew what he was talking about. So he kept his eyes open, and looked sharp, as the painter had advised. Soon he found a steady job. And rather odd it was, too.

Every day either Eben or Jerry carried a pail of Pansy's milk to Mrs. Hill, who lived beyond the Sawyers. She had a white poodle named Trixy.

"I heard you tell my Granzie you wished you had somebody to wash your dog," Eben announced one evening at Mrs. Hill's door.

Mrs. Hill took the pail from Eben. "Why, bless you, so I did. Do you think you could bathe my little Trixy?"

"Yes, I do," answered Eben, stoutly, "if you would show me how."

"It's a bargain," agreed Mrs. Hill, "if you prove you can do it. I'll pay you twenty cents if you will come every Saturday morning. I do like Trixy to be fresh as a daisy for Sundays."

Twenty cents! Eben had expected at least thirty. Maybe fifty. He shuffled his feet. "Uh—excuse me for saying it," he stammered, "but do you s'pose you could make it twenty-five cents? That would exactly buy one whole war stamp."

"War stamps, is it?" Mrs. Hill screwed up her mouth in study. "We-ell, all right," she said at last, and her mouth came back to its proper shape. "Five cents more a week won't hurt me, I guess." She looked down at Eben rather sternly.

"When I was a little girl, Eben Tuttle, children scarcely ever had a nickel of their own to spend. Twenty-five cents would have seemed a fortune to them. And we were just as happy as you modern children are, mind you, with all your weekly allowances and your pay for doing chores that we did for nothing. Times have changed, and I don't know," reflected Mrs. Hill, looking off into space, "I really don't know which system is best."

Eben's mind was on the present, and not on those long-ago days when such a bleak and unfair system prevailed. And in spite of thinking that

[92]

Mrs. Hill might well have offered him a higher rate for making her poodle "as fresh as a daisy," he walked home feeling rather like a businessman going home to supper after making a big deal. "After all," he consoled himself, "a poodle is much smaller than a cow."

Every Saturday, after that, Eben bathed the white poodle. Trixy hated the soap and water. She would scuttle off and hide under the davenport when she saw Eben coming. He took to romping with her, first, so that she would like him better. Then, in the midst of their fun, and much to her surprise, he would pick her up and carry her off to her bath. After she was washed and rubbed between towels, she was as fluffy as spun candy. She would tear around like mad, huffing at Eben, and daring him to catch her. He taught her to shake hands, which pleased Mrs. Hill so much that she actually gave him an extra quarter. Eben rushed

[93]

to the post-office and bought a war stamp while the quarter was still warm from Mrs. Hill's hand. After all, bathing pretty little Trixy was a very pleasant way to earn even so small an amount as twenty-five cents a week.

The tie was helping like everything, too. He was doing so well that Mother allowed him to go to Wicker's Field every Saturday afternoon, besides practicing three times a week with the Bearcats, between school and milking-time. Eben was being extra kind to his little brothers. He helped Roy the handy man to spade and plant the garden, and to mow the lawn. He and Jerry gathered the eggs for Granzie, and never broke a single one.

And in spite of simply hating his part in a patriotic pageant for which Miss Jennings was drilling the children for the last of school, Eben went through it bravely. It was a sissy part, he thought, and why didn't Miss Jennings give it to Peaches

Bradley, who, instead, had one of the bravest and best rôles? Mother understood how he felt about the part, but not about Peaches Bradley. She called him a good trooper, which was very cheering. And Granzie said, "Eben is like my father, Ebenezer. I declare, just see who is man-of-the-house now!"

That made little Jerry want to do his best, too. Jerry was being as good as gold.

All of the teachers and visiting parents said that the patriotic pageant was splendid. After school closed the pupils gave a public performance in the lodge hall, and charged admission. Only two or three people in Sidneyville were mean enough to say that they had already seen it once, free, so why pay to see it again? A nice profit was made for the Red Cross, and all the children were very proud.

Soon it was too hot to wear anything but a pair of shorts. Father's tie was impossible. Granzie cleaned it, and hung it over the electric fixture in

Eben's room. Mother gave a sigh of relief to see it there, instead of around Eben's neck.

One morning Granzie had a more bustling air than usual. "Today I am going to clean out my room, and give it the scouring of its life," she announced. "Roy is so busy. It will be days before he can help us finish our spring cleaning. But I don't mind," Granzie tossed her head like an old warhorse. "I like to work," she declared. "I love to make things shine. What's more, I am old-fashioned enough to want my rugs out on the grass, to sun and air. Poor things, they never get out!" Granzie laughed, and her eyes gleamed at the prospect of working so hard.

"So, Eben, my boy," almost sang Granzie, "you may help me carry the rugs downstairs and out to the yard."

Eben hated to dash Granzie's high spirits. But it couldn't be helped. "Chuckie Howard and I are

[96]

going to dig fishin' worms this morning," he said. "There he comes, now. A fellow can't work ALL the time!" he added, seeing that Granzie did not look the least dashed.

"I won't keep you long, dear," promised Granzie, sweetly. "Chuckie won't mind waiting."

And Mother said, "Think how often Granzie helps you, Son."

Yes, that was perfectly true. "You sit here on the side steps and wait, Chuckie," advised Eben. "I'll hurry like blazes."

While Chuckie waited, Eben helped Granzie to empty her room. It was rather fun, shoving the helpless dresser and table and chairs around and crowding them into a corner of the upper hall. Great-grandfather Ebenezer was unhung, and laid face down on some papers on the dresser.

"There, now!" exclaimed Granzie, cheerily, "you will soon be through. You may roll up these

smaller rugs and carry them down while I am collecting my cleaning materials. Roll up the hall
runner, too. But don't try to carry it down by yourself, dear. You are not strong enough."

"Shucks!" said Eben, when Granzie had tripped
downstairs. He flexed his arm. What other boy,
especially such a skinny boy, had a harder muscle?
He would show Granzie how strong he was. He
would surprise her.

He would show Chuckie, too. Eben snorted with
glee. Chuckie—chatting quietly with Jerry on the
steps below Granzie's window—what a big surprise he was going to have! Eben would not only
prove his strength and play a good joke, but he
would save a lot of time. Granzie had often declared that if people would only use their brains,
they could easily invent ways of saving themselves
time and labor. "Make short work of work," said
Granzie.

[98]

Eben wound up the hall runner in a loose, careless roll. It was heavier than he had guessed. But not too heavy for a boy with muscle, of course. Kicking the small rugs in Granzie's room out of the way, he dragged the runner over to the open window. He lifted one end, gave the other a shove and a heave. It balanced on the sill, half in and half out. Eben gave it a mighty push. He could see it sailing out into space. Jiminy! This was much easier than carrying the rugs downstairs, one by one. Yes, siree, this was certainly a short cut!

Eben snatched up one of the small rugs. But first he would see what Chuckie thought of this clever way of making short work of work. He peered over the sill. His eyes widened and stared. He hung there, half out of the window, stiff with surprise.

Below, on the path leading around to the side steps, lay the hall runner. But it was alive! It was crawling and heaving. Strange noises were coming from under it. Grunts and hisses and gasps. Now it reared up like an animal. A claw—no, a human hand appeared. A bare arm. An arm streaked with bright red!

Eben scrambled to his feet. He rushed downstairs and out the side door. And there, shaking off the rug and standing up, was—a boy Eben knew! He didn't look like himself. Still, that's who it was. Peaches Bradley!

Peaches' bare chest was smeared horribly with the same wet, gory stain. His fingers were dripping with it. What on earth! Eben stared, openmouthed and fearful.

But now Peaches was advancing, slowly. Crouched, like a tiger about to spring. His eyes burned blue as flames. Eben took a step backward. He was not afraid, of course. But who had ever

It was alive! It was crawling and heaving.

seen Peaches Bradley look like this? Cripes, maybe Peaches wasn't such a sissy, after all!

"I didn't do it on purpose, Peaches," shouted Eben, bracing himself. "I didn't know you were there. Not anywhere near."

Peaches hesitated. His head whirled around, like that of a startled owl. Was that Jerry, creeping up on him from the rear?

But Jerry had only one thought. He wanted to see what was under that rug. There was something very mysterious under that rug. Maybe something dead under that rug. Jerry kicked it back with his toe, cautiously. The boys stared.

On the path lay all that was left of a strawberry pie. It had been a magnificent pie. One could see that. A pie of pies! Now it had fallen from the pan. It was completely ruined. Scarlet juice oozed over the walk. The crust was broken and shattered.

Jerry looked gravely at these sad remains. "It was a pie," he stated.

And suddenly something happened to Peaches. His fists undoubled. His face cleared. He grinned at Eben. He began to laugh.

"The pie was a present for your grandmother," explained Peaches, "because Mother says she's such a good Sunday-school teacher. The pie and I, well, we got here just as the rug did."

Then all the boys laughed. They rolled on the grass, laughing. They couldn't help it, even though it was too bad about the delicious strawberry pie. To think of Peaches being knocked flat by the rug, just as it fell to earth! It was better than a comic. They shrieked, remembering how the rug had crawled about on the path. They howled to see how Peaches was smeared with juice. Red, bright red! They laughed until they ached all over to see Peaches making a monkey of himself, licking the red juice off his fingers and wrists. Why, Peaches Bradley was a cut-up! Peaches was a good sport! Peaches was a regular fellow!

"Want to dig fishin' worms with me and Chuckie, Peaches?" asked Eben.

"Okay," answered Peaches.

But Granzie and Mother didn't think it was the least funny to lose that fine pie. The pie that Mrs. Bradley had made with such loving care for her Sunday-school teacher. "Strawberries—my sakes alive, they are so scarce and expensive this year," breathed Granzie, *so* disappointed.

Nor did Mother and Granzie think it had been the least clever of Eben to try to save time by throwing the rugs out of the window. They said it was a lazy way of working. "Haste makes waste," said Granzie. Which was strange, as it seemed the exact opposite from what she had said about short cuts.

Eben soon discovered that it was going to take him a long time to undo what he had done, though of course he could do nothing about the pie. Nobody could. "You and Peaches run along now and dig your fishing worms without Eben," said Mother to Chuckie. "Eben must shovel up the remains of the pie, and use the hose on the walk. He must scrub off the worst of the stain on the rug. He must carry the other rugs down for Granzie. It will take him quite a while," said Mother. "Come in now, Peaches, and wash yourself. All that horrible, sticky red! And don't tell your mother. Not yet. It wasn't your fault. I'll tell her myself, later."

Chuckie and Peaches walked off presently without a word, and Jerry with them. They did not look back once. Fellows don't do that to a pal who is in trouble. A pal who was finding it not at all easy to be man-of-the-house. "No wonder," complained Eben. "I didn't have on the tie."

But Mother said again, very firmly, that the necktie had nothing to do with it. And it was a strange thing, but soon after that the black-and-orange tie disappeared. Just as the other one had mysteriously vanished, the green one with the liver-colored spots.

IX

What's in a Name?

SOMEHOW, after the day that Eben threw the rug out of the upper window and smashed the strawberry pie, Granzie did not boast that he was like her side of the family. She never said any more that he was the very image of Great-grandfather Ebenezer. Neither Granzie nor Mother called him man-of-the-house. Not even the *young* man-of-the-house. Nothing was said about it, one way or the other. It seemed quite forgotten. Eben almost forgot about it himself. But sometimes at night, before he went to sleep and was thinking about Father, he remembered the feel of that kind, firm hand on his shoulder, and what Father had said at the railroad station. Then Eben squirmed and tossed in his bed, and wished he could see Father and talk things over.

But since Father was far away, and since there seemed to be no more of his neckties that Eben could wear, he decided there was no use trying any more. He would be—just a boy. That kept him flying about as nimbly as a squirrel.

And all the more nimbly because of Peaches Bradley. Eben had discovered that in spite of those big blue eyes and that girly complexion, Peaches was a regular fellow. A boy full of adventure and bright ideas. As smart as a whip was Peaches. It seemed strange indeed, but now Eben and Peaches were the best of friends. Eben wrote to Father about it. But not about the rug and the strawberry pie. That would have been un-cheerful news.

"I used to think Peaches was a sissy," wrote Eben. "But he's okay. We work for the high-school team together now. I've got him with the

Bearcats, too. And boy, can he run! Peaches has a swell collection of war posters, Father. They are tacked up in his room, and in the upper hall. I do think it is super of mothers to let a boy like Peaches use a house for things like that. Don't you?"

Father answered Eben's letter, and agreed. And he said, "About you and Peaches, that's the way things sometimes happen. It is a fine thing to make such a discovery. You learn that underneath the look and manner you thought you didn't like, there is a real person. It gives one a good feeling —a feeling of warm and happy surprise and satisfaction. Like discovering treasure. There's a fellow like that in my unit. At first I thought he was a pain in the neck. Now we are buddies, like you and Peaches."

Peaches made the summer seem more alive and busy than other summers. He had not only collected war posters, but in his round blond head there was tucked away an amazing amount of information from the books he had read. He could talk about the various admirals and generals and rulers as intimately as if they were members of the Bearcats. Islands and harbors and cities and battle-fields—their names rolled glibly off of Peaches' tongue. He knew everything, it seemed to Eben, about airplanes. He said he would be an aviator someday. Eben didn't doubt it.

If that was what reading did for a fellow—was it sissy, after all? Eben and Peaches had a fine time sprawled on the grass, or on the floor of Peaches' room, studying the maps in books that Peaches owned, or had borrowed from the Public Library. They talked and argued by the hour. "I should think you and Peaches would wear blisters on your tongues," laughed Mother. "I never heard such talkers."

But she was pleased. "Boys and girls should

learn all they can," she said, "for they are the future citizens of the world. Perhaps you and Peaches and Chuckie may someday be flying to Australia or China or Iran or Russia as a matter of course, being friends and working with people of other lands. How wonderful that day will be—when all men are brothers!" Mother's eyes shone.

Peaches went with Eben when he drove Pansy to pasture and back, so they wouldn't have to stop talking. And since Peaches had showed Eben his war posters and his books and maps, Eben showed Pansy's illustrious pedigree to Peaches and to Chuckie. They were much impressed.

"*Trumpeter, Island Ruler, Silver Comet,*" read Peaches. "Those are swell names. Those cows must have been supers." He was silent a moment. "Ever notice how everything has to have a name?" he asked. "Wonder how people's names ever got

[112]

started. Wonder what they meant in the first place."

That was the kind of a person Peaches was—always trying to learn the reasons for things.

"What's your real name, Peaches?" asked Eben, suddenly. "I can't remember what it was before your aunt said—"

"It's Owen," answered Peaches. "Owen Algernon Bradley."

"Help!" giggled Chuckie. "That doesn't mean anything."

"Means as much as Chuckie, I guess," argued Peaches.

"Charles," corrected Chuckie. "Charles Howard."

"Well, what does that mean?" demanded Peaches, to pay Chuckie back.

"Dunno. Nothing, I guess," admitted Chuckie.

[113]

"You will find your names in the back part of the dictionary, boys," called Granzie from the sitting-room. "Look them up under *Christian Names of Men,* and stop arguing. I can't read."

The boys rushed to Father's big dictionary. They riffled its pages with well-moistened thumbs. "Here 'tis," cried Peaches, pouncing. He looked up his name first, naturally.

Owen = lamb: young warrior. So the dictionary informed Peaches.

"Huh, how could you be a lamb and a young warrior at the same time? They're different," scoffed Chuckie.

"I s'pose it means you can choose whichever you like the best," said Peaches. "If you want to be a lamb, you can be a lamb. If you want to be a young warrior, you can be a young warrior. I choose 'young warrior.' "

[114]

"Now let's see what 'Charles' means," cried Chuckie, trying to edge Peaches aside.

"In a minute." Peaches planted himself more firmly in front of the dictionary stand. "Might as well finish me first. Algernon—that's my middle name."

"Algernon = with whiskers," read Peaches. Eben and Chuckie cast questioning glances at his smooth cheeks.

" 'With whiskers,' " murmured Eben. "Like Uncle Sam. Like Great-grandfather Ebenezer."

"A lamb with whiskers!" Chuckie dug his elbow into Peaches' side, teasing.

"Young warrior with whiskers, you mean." Peaches wouldn't be teased.

Chuckie swelled out his chest when he discovered that a boy named Charles was bound to be "strong, manly, noble-spirited." It was not quite so definitely splendid as being a young warrior, but it had fine possibilities.

Now it was Eben's turn. His name was not to be found. In vain, three rather soiled fingernails went up and down the columns of the E's. "Maybe Eben's not a Christian name," suggested Peaches.

Suddenly Eben remembered that his name was really Ebenezer.

"Ebenezer!" shouted Chuckie and Peaches. "Help! Is *that* your real name? Ebenezer is a geezer," rhymed Chuckie.

"Ebenezer is a sneezer," giggled Peaches.

"Ebenezer = stone of help," read Eben from the dictionary. His forehead puckered. It was like a riddle. How could a stone help? A stone was for carrying in one's pocket. A little mottled one, worn smooth and round, and pleasant to roll between one's fingers. Or for skipping across the pond

[116]

north of town, if you could bring yourself to giving it up. *Stone of help*—how silly!

Eben felt irked while the boys searched hilariously for the meaning of their friends' names, and for those who were not their friends. Why couldn't he have been named Orson, for instance? *Orson = a bear.* Or *Napoleon, lion of the forest dell.* Or *Rolf, famous wolf.* Or, shoot the luck, even *Island Ruler!*

He talked it over with Granzie that evening. "Names are scarcely ever selected for children because of what they actually mean," explained Granzie. "Parents don't bother to look them up in the dictionary. You were named for your great-grandfather, as fine a man as ever walked this earth. *Ebenezer*—it comes from the Bible, as do so many of our names." When Eben and Jerry were in bed, Granzie told them the story from the Bible.

[117]

"The Israelites went into battle against the Philistines. They camped beside a place called Ebenezer," began Granzie.

"Who beat?" asked Jerry.

"The Philistines," answered Granzie. "Moreover, after the victory, they stole the Ark of the Lord, and carried it away. To the Israelites the Ark of the Lord was the most sacred thing in all the world. It was a box, inlaid and lined with pure gold. It contained the laws of the Israelites which had been given to them by Moses—the sacred tablets. And other precious things as well. Usually the Ark of the Lord was kept in the temple. But the Israelites had brought it into battle because they thought it would save them from the Philistines.

"So for many years the sacred Ark was gone from its holy place in the temple. The Israelites mourned for it. At last the prophet Samuel told them that God would deliver them from the Phi-

[118]

listines and restore the Ark to them, if they would put away their strange gods and serve the Lord only.

"So the Israelites destroyed their gods that were nothing but images of brass. Then there was another great battle with the Philistines. And the Bible says, 'The Lord thundered with a great thunder on that day upon the Philistines, and they were smitten before Israel.'

"To celebrate their victory, the Israelites set up a stone. They called the stone *Ebenezer* in memory of that place where they had been defeated by the Philistines so many years before. All the cities they had lost were restored to them, and there was peace.

"*Ebenezer*—an ancient name, out of ancient times," mused Granzie. "A strong name, as strong as stone. It suited your great-grandfather."

Even if his name did rhyme with *geezer* and

[119]

sneezer, Eben thought better of it than ever he had. But after Granzie had kissed the boys good night and turned out the light, Eben gave a little sigh. Wasn't a great deal expected of him? Not only Father and Mother, if they had not forgotten, expected him to be man-of-the-house. But now Great-grandfather Ebenezer, and maybe Uncle Sam, too, thought Eben, half-asleep, expected him to be a *stone of help.*

X

Aunt May and Her Dog

EBEN and Chuckie and Peaches talked about
Dogs for Defense. Eben wished he had a beloved
dog to give, with willing hands, but aching heart,
to one of the services. What a terrific wrench that
would be! But brave and patriotic, thought Eben.
"The only thing," he told his friends, "I don't have
a dog. If Trixy were the right kind, I bet I could
persuade Mrs. Hill to give her up."

And the next time that Eben bathed Trixy he
felt quite put out with her, because she was not
useful, but only a pretty member of dog society.

"We have Bozo," said Chuckie, "but he's too
old." The boys couldn't help laughing at the

thought of stiff, sleepy old Bozo trying to be a Dog for Defense.

"My Aunt May over in Edenburn has a police dog," said Chuckie.

"He ought to go to war," declared Eben.

"Sure he ought," agreed Peaches.

"Sure," said Chuckie.

The three boys went to see Mr. Sawyer, who had a painting job over in Edenburn. "Could we ride to the county seat with you when you go tomorrow?" they chorused.

"I don't mind, if your mothers say so," said Mr. Sawyer.

The next morning the boys hopped out of Mr. Sawyer's car at the corner nearest Aunt May's house in Edenburn. Chuckie's cheeks were so red with excitement that his freckles had almost disappeared. He rang the bell. At once the door popped open. It was so unexpectedly sudden that the boys jumped.

"Hi, Aunt—Aunt May!" stammered Chuckie. "I have come to visit you."

"I see you have," answered Aunt May. "And two others so nearly like you I can scarcely tell you apart."

The boys laughed, politely. Surely Aunt May had very bad eyes. Because Chuckie had red hair and freckles, Eben was as brown as a gypsy, and Peaches, well, it could not be helped, but Peaches had a complexion like peaches-and-cream.

Aunt May went on. "All boys look alike to me. However, come in. Will you be here for lunch?"

"Sure," answered Chuckie. "I mean, we might be. I mean—if you don't want us, you *could* send us home on the bus. Only we don't have the money for the bus fare. 'Cause, naturally, we planned to stay all day with you, and ride back free with Mr. Sawyer."

"We'll go to the cafeteria for lunch," said Aunt May. "I couldn't hope to cook enough to fill three boys. Not with rationing the way it is."

"*Boy!* The cafeteria!" cried Chuckie. He grinned at his friends, proud to show them that he had an aunt who would take them to a cafeteria.

Eben and Peaches were thrilled, too. Only they were just a little afraid of Aunt May, who spoke so plainly. But they had come on an important patriotic mission, and it was time they were getting around to it.

"D'you have a dog?" asked Eben.

"You heard him barking his head off as you came up the walk," answered Aunt May. "He's chained to his kennel. His name is Scout. He's rather fierce with strangers."

[124]

"I told you he's that kind of a dog," whispered Chuckie.

"Perhaps we might sit on the back porch where Scout can see you," suggested Aunt May. "When he gets used to you, and has decided that you are not bandits, he will be more friendly. Then you can play with him."

So they sat on the porch, quietly. Scout could see, surely, that they were respectable boys, and not bandits. Aunt May invited them to help themselves to a small bowl of salted peanuts. She inquired after Chuckie's parents and his sisters. "How much canned goods did your mother put up?" she asked.

Chuckie thought—and chewed—very hard. "A lot," he answered.

After that nobody could think of a thing to say, it seemed. That was extremely odd, because what the boys had in mind was fairly burning to be said. But how would they begin? How would Aunt May take it? Eben and Peaches frowned at Chuckie and made signs with their thumbs. He was the one to start the thing going, for Pete's sake. This lady was *his* aunt. And wasn't Scout practically Chuckie's cousin?

Chuckie fidgeted. He made several false starts as the precious moments sped by.

"This is a very patriotic time of world, isn't it?" ventured Eben, at last. He blushed, because what he had said didn't quite make sense, after all.

But Aunt May understood, and agreed. She asked the boys what they were doing these days that was patriotic. They told her with a rush, all talking at once. Eben managed to shout the loudest when he informed Aunt May that his father was a captain. "But a doctor at the same time."

As soon as Aunt May discovered how much these Sidneyville boys knew about planes and tanks and

[126]

guns and ships and generals and admirals, she settled back in her chair. She said it was as good as being at field headquarters, and "in the know." She said she wished to goodness she were a young man, and lucky enough to be a soldier. "It's stuffy," said Aunt May, "not being in the very thick of it."

"You could be, Aunt May," cried Eben, eagerly. "I mean—" Now what was Aunt May's other name?

"Call me Aunt May if you like," she said. "But how could I be in the thick of it, young man?"

"Maybe not exactly," admitted Eben. "But pretty nearly. Because you'd be sacrificing something for your country." He took a deep breath. "You would hate like everything giving up your dog, wouldn't you?"

"Of course I would," answered Aunt May, tartly. "But why should I? Don't tell me you boys

[127]

came all the way to Edenburn to ask me to give Scout to you!"

"Not to us, Aunt May," cried Chuckie, full of courage at last. "But to your country. You see we haven't any dog to give to Dogs for Defense. So we thought of you as next best. Maybe—"

Aunt May stared at her three visitors. She threw back her head and laughed. People as far as the fourth house down the street might have heard Aunt May laughing. And Scout got up, turned around, and lay down again, uneasily.

But right away Aunt May had to straighten her face, for the boys were looking at her as shocked as if she had cackled out in church.

"I see what you mean, boys," she said, soberly. "And I'll be switched if it wouldn't be a good idea. Perhaps I could help in that way, Scout and I. It will be lonesome, but—"

The boys crowded close to Aunt May's chair.

[128]

"You will get him back when the war's over," crooned Eben, gently.

"And then he will be a better dog than ever, Aunt May," assured Chuckie.

"You're *regular*, Aunt May," complimented Peaches.

"Thank you, boys," smiled Aunt May. "I feel like old man Job, in the Bible, being comforted by his three good friends, Eliphaz, Bildad, and Zophar. I shall inquire at once, and if Scout qualifies, he shall go to war. Now let's tell him about it."

Scout seemed to like tremendously the thought of going to war. The air was filled with a hulla-baloo of ear-splitting barks when Aunt May un-chained him and said, "Scout, how would you like to be a Defense dog for your Uncle Sam?" He leaped about, fawning upon Aunt May, and lick-ing the boys' cheeks. They had to brace themselves with all their strength, to keep from being knocked

[129]

down, for Scout was taller than any of them when he stood on his hind legs. "He sure will make a good Defense dog," agreed the boys, happily.

After they had played with Scout, or rather, after Scout had played with them, they washed their hands, at Aunt May's suggestion. And even their faces. She took them down town. "I must stop at the bank for a moment," she told them. "Yonder is the cafeteria, the Busy Bee. You may go in and begin selecting what you would like to eat. Within reason, of course," warned Aunt May. "I shall join you soon."

To be turned loose in a cafeteria! It was marvelous! The boys shoved their trays along the counter. Chuckie went first and set the example, because he was Aunt May's own nephew.

Who wanted salads? Nobody. There were better things ahead. Each boy took a huge square of cornbread and a fat muffin. *Two* pats of butter. The

[130]

baked ham and brown gravy and sweet potatoes—
yummy—to pass them by was not "within reason."
Their tongues fairly hung out as they gazed at the
whitefish and the baked Idahos. "Hot air!" exclaimed Chuckie, flushed and reckless, "we'll take
'em all!"

By the time the boys had ordered baked hash,
green beans, roasting ears, and two desserts apiece,
Aunt May appeared. "Heavens!" she cried. "It
would have been cheaper to have sent you home
on the bus before lunch. Much cheaper. I wonder," said Aunt May, turning to the checker,
"what the hungry children of Europe and Asia
would think of these trays. I even wonder what
Uncle Sam would think of his three young
patriots."

The boys blushed and shuffled their feet. "We
forgot," they murmured.

"Well, it's too late now," declared Aunt May.

[131]

"So stagger along with your trays. I suppose you will need a lot of body-building food if you are to be future good citizens."

But then Aunt May and the checker began to worry for fear the boys would crumple under the weight of their trays, and break all the Busy Bee dishes, which Aunt May would have to pay for. Not to mention the mess. Two waitresses sprang to the beck and call of the checker. One took Eben's tray. The other took Peaches', while those two lads followed, taking long steps, swinging their arms, and feeling carefree.

"Now, Charles," said Aunt May to Chuckie, "you carry mine. I'll carry yours. Goo-ood-*NESS!*" she cried, as she picked up Chuckie's tray. She set it down, while she shifted her purse, straightened her hat, and took a deep breath. Then she started off with the loaded salver, shuffling along as if among eggs, and with her mouth sucked in and her

Louis Slobodkin

The boys staggered along with their trays.

eyes bulging. They bulged partly because it was all she could do to carry Chuckie's monstrous lunch. And partly because the pot of tea, with its cup-and-saucer, and the lone sandwich which she had selected for her own refreshment, were skidding merrily to and fro on the tray borne by Chuckie. "Look what you're doing, Charles!" panted Aunt May.

But Chuckie didn't seem to hear. Chuckie was treating Aunt May's tray with artful indifference. He was wearing a small, embarrassed smile. His hair seemed more red than usual, his freckles larger. For Chuckie was pretending not to care should anyone happen to be watching him. But— *good night,* EVERYBODY in the Busy Bee would think that he, husky pitcher for the Bearcats, could eat nothing but a little old dry sandwich and a tiny pot of tea! *TEA!*

All in all, it was quite a procession, and the Busy

[135]

Bee had never seemed busier than at this moment. Finally the trays were unloaded and whisked away by the giggling waitresses. Peace descended, and the boys forgot everything but the joy of eating.

But when they filed out of the cafeteria, Aunt May was carrying home to Scout a whopping mound of baked hash. She hadn't smiled a bit as she scraped it, almost untouched, off the boys' plates into a paper boat borrowed from the Busy Bee. But her three guests knew what she was thinking — that they were thoughtless, unpatriotic greedies—and they felt ashamed as they followed meekly down the street. It was most consoling to see how heartily Scout enjoyed the baked hash. And by the time Mr. Sawyer called for the boys, they were once more on the best of terms with Aunt May.

"Be sure and let us know if Scout goes to war,"

[136]

urged Chuckie, as they said good-by. "Maybe we'll come back and see you when the County Fair opens."

"There isn't going to be any County Fair this year," said Aunt May. "But thank you, my three countrymen, for coming and reminding me and Scout of our duty."

"Oh, that's okay," grinned the boys modestly. "We didn't mind."

Going home in the car they bounced about among Mr. Sawyer's paint-buckets, telling him of Scout. "Dog-bite-it!" exclaimed Mr. Sawyer, over and over. Nothing could have been more fitting.

But the boys were stunned at what Aunt May had said about the Fair. "No County Fair!" they grumbled. "Shoot the luck!"

"We have to give up a good many usual things now, and without whining," reminded Mr.

[137]

Sawyer. "No County Fair on account of gas rationing, you know. And then of course the farmers are too busy producing precious food. Everyone is too busy."

XI

Come to the Fair

EBEN and Peaches and Chuckie decided to have a Fair of their own. "All the money we make we'll give to the Red Cross," declared Eben.

"Where shall we hold the Fair?" asked Chuckie. That was a problem. But at last Mr. Sawyer offered to store the Tuttle automobile, so that the boys could hold the Fair in the garage that would then be empty. Though later, as the Fair grew, it overflowed into the drive and even into the yard.

The boys flushed the garage with the garden hose and scrubbed the floor with brooms. They could scarcely wait for it to dry. Three of Peaches' biggest war posters were tacked on the walls. Mr. Sawyer made some long trestles. On these were

[139]

arranged the exhibits, mostly vegetables. Fine red tomatoes, scrubbed carrots, beets and beans and corn out of the Bradley, Howard, and Tuttle gardens.

But before that, Mr. Sawyer had made what he called a sandwich board. He made it of two strips of beaver board the same size and fastened together at the top with pieces of leather run through holes. Jerry was the fat little sandwich. The boards hung from his shoulders, one at the front and one at the back. Jerry walked between the boards up and down the streets of Sidneyville, advertising the Fair. He was as proud as a king and as happy as a honeybee. The green letters on the boards said:

COME TO THE FAIR
at
The Tuttle Garage
Benefit of the Red Cross

It was really surprising how many people came to the Fair. Not only every boy and girl in Sidneyville, but a great many grown-ups. The druggist's wife donated all-day suckers and in turn bought carrots. The grocer gave a dozen rare bananas and bought the peanut cookies that Granzie had made. Mrs. Sawyer bought back all the tomatoes that Mr. Sawyer had carried over when she wasn't looking. She was in the midst of canning tomatoes.

Mrs. Hill gave two glasses of jelly. They were snapped up and paid for before anyone had a chance to see whether they were raspberry or currant, or *what* kind of jelly. The postmaster and the ticket man at the railroad station came to chuckle and to buy. Old Doctor Draper dropped in. He said he had nothing to donate except pills and castor oil, and they never seemed popular, somehow. "So here is a dollar for your Red Cross fund," said the doctor.

Florabelle Marshall, who was in Eben's grade at school, came and looked things over. "Hm-m-m, you haven't any flowers," she said. "There are always flowers at Fairs." Florabelle made an offer. She said that she and her chum Marylou would collect bouquets if they would be allowed to arrange and sell them. Before long one side of the garage was gay with cannas that were like scarlet flames. With coxcomb that were like ruffled red velvet. With gladiolas and zinnias and marigolds and asters. They sold for ten and fifteen cents a bunch, and the little girls who sold them were quite as pretty as the flowers themselves. Only the boys didn't notice.

"We ought to have a livestock exhibit, too," declared Peaches.

The livestock exhibit was just for show. Because of course you couldn't sell Pansy and Bozo and Trixy. You couldn't even sell chances on them. Though Fred Goff, the druggist, offered one thousand dollars and ninety-eight cents for Pansy. He pounded on the trestle and said in a loud, fierce voice that he *would* have Pansy, whether or no. Eben was scared. But Mother laughed and said, "Don't you know that Fred Goff is the biggest tease in town?"

The animals made a hullabaloo of noise. Trixy and Bozo, securely tied, barked madly at each other, and at Pansy and at the rooster and four hens from Granzie's flock, and at the goat the boys had borrowed from Florabelle's grandfather. When Florabelle's cat and old Mrs. Arnold's parrot were added to the exhibit, Bozo and Trixy launched into a perfect frenzy of barking. The rooster crowed. The parrot and the hens squawked. The cat spit and arched her back. The goat baa-ed and pawed the grass with his sharp hoofs, and Pansy switched her usually amiable tail,

[143]

furiously. She looked almost as fierce as her ancestor, *Stampede,* must have looked.

A thunderstorm blew up. There was a wild scramble getting the livestock unfastened and led to shelter, Pansy into her stall, the chickens back to the henhouse, the cat into the back porch, and Bozo dragged into the garage. Mrs. Hill came flying to the rescue of Trixy, carrying her pet homeward in her arms, and murmuring foolish baby-talk. There was nothing to do about the goat until the storm was over. The wind and the rain and lightning—alas, the poor old billy-goat had to endure them!

That was the end of the livestock exhibit, except for Jerry's spiders and worms he had long been collecting and preserving in bottles of alcohol. There were always two or three Sidneyville boys staring at Jerry's collection. Jerry would not have sold them for anything. Not even for the benefit of the Red Cross.

But one day, in a moment of zeal, Chuckie sold Jerry's most precious item. It was a big, fat tomato worm. He sold it to a boy named Jimmy Crane. Five cents for the worm, and ten cents for the nice bottle of alcohol in which the worm appeared as green and plump as ever it had on the vine.

In spite of being told over and over that he and the worm had done their noble bit toward the Red Cross, Jerry cried and cried. "There, there!" soothed Granzie, "whoever heard of such grief over a worm!" She searched her own and the neighbors' tomato vines until she had found another worm for Jerry. It was even bigger and better than the one sold to Jimmy Crane. Jerry was happy again.

Florabelle and Marylou insisted on a baby show.

[145]

"Of all the crazy ideas!" scoffed the boys. But Florabelle and Marylou kept talking about it.

"Who started this Fair, anyhow?" demanded the boys. "And you can't sell babies. Or can you?"

"Of course not," said Florabelle. "But all the women in town would come to see the babies, wouldn't they? And there would be your chance to sell a lot of other things, wouldn't it?"

"That's an idea," admitted the boys. "But we're not going to look after the babies. How many would you have?"

"A lot of them," promised Florabelle and Marylou. "Just leave it to us."

But they could round up only four babies, after all. There was Joey, the eldest, and the only man in the lot. Joey had on his best rompers, tight, because he was outgrowing them. Pale pink they were, with the pockets and collar embroidered in tiny forget-me-nots. In spite of this dainty garment, Joey was looking like a hooligan in a white cotton painter's cap of Mr. Sawyer's. If you walked slowly around Joe, you could read the words printed on the cap. "Buy Your Paints at Binger's Hardware, Edenburn."

Florabelle had donated her sister. There were two other baby girls. Each was in its own play pen. All of the babies were awarded blue ribbons, because, as Marylou said, "They are as cute as each other." And of course no one wanted to be partial, no matter what they privately thought.

There was no doubt that Florabelle and Marylou knew the tricks of business. They had advised the boys to sell food on this last day of the Fair, and had helped to collect it. Because the baby show did indeed attract many women, the baked beans and potato salad and fresh bread and cookies and other good things found a ready sale. Jerry and his best chum sold lemonade.

[147]

There was even some needlework for sale. Among the aprons and pot-holders and embroidered towels appeared Granzie's crocheted tablemat. Mother bought it at once. She tucked it under her arm with a small, tender smile. It was strange, but Mother paid two dollars for the mat that Granzie had made from those gaudy ties Mother had not liked at all.

The *Sidneyville Caller* printed an account of the Fair. An item appeared in the county paper, too. Aunt May saw it. She wrote Chuckie a letter. She said that Scout had already gone to war, and that she felt sure he would be a hero and come home with a medal. And she enclosed a check for five dollars to add to the Red Cross fund. She said that of course she had to sign the check, but that it was really from their friend Scout. The boys swelled with pride and a sense of well-doing.

[148]

It was hard to settle down to school. And if Eben had not been in the house long enough to be the man of it, or even a "stone of help," at least he had been a busy and patriotic boy out of it.

XII

While the Town Slept

ABOUT the middle of October there came a letter from Father that made the days seem more golden and the sky more blue. Football seemed more exciting than ever before, and the Tuttle house rang with joy and laughter. Eben went whistling off to school each morning, and came home every evening, whistling. Jerry couldn't whistle a tune yet, but he sang "Your Flag and My Flag," and "God Bless America" at the top of his voice. As Granzie fed the chickens or made the beds her deep strong voice could be heard singing, "A Mighty Fortress is Our God." Mother sang, too. But generally she went about the house, not saying much, but as if she were preparing for some

[150]

happy festival, a light in her eyes and her step quick and springy. Joey tried to sing. The noise he made was not exactly musical, but very jolly.

Roy the handy man gave Pansy's stable, and the Jersey herself, such a cleaning as had never been done before. Some of Father's friends chipped in and bought a new curry-brush for Pansy, with her name on it in gold—"Pansy the Third."

For Father's letter had said, "I'm not absolutely sure yet, but I think Uncle Sam may give me a short leave. Maybe in time for Mother's birthday." Wasn't that enough to make everyone in the family sing and whistle?

Jerry went into Granzie's room. "Thank you, Uncle Sam," he said to Great-grandfather Ebenezer, "for letting my father come home." But then he remembered, and ducked out, feeling foolish. Those whiskers again!

As for Eben, he began to think of all the things

he wanted to tell Father, and to show him. Such as his war-stamp book that Trixy and Pansy were helping to fill. He began to wonder if Father would feel very much let down when he learned that his eldest son had not always been man-of-the-house. So seldom, in fact, that everyone except Eben had forgotten.

Even if it turned out that Father had not forgotten, and still expected manly things of Eben, it would be good to talk things over. Father and Eben would get these serious matters over as soon as possible, to make room for the swell stories and pillow-fights, besides all the hours Father would want to spend with Mother and Granzie and his friends.

Mother's birthday was November the twelfth. On the sixth, Eben received a letter from Father. It was marked "personal," which meant that no one must read it but Eben. He took it to his room, and locked the door.

"Dear Son," wrote Father. "In case I should not arrive for Mother's birthday, here is a check. You are to order some flowers from McBean the florist. Yellow roses if possible. I would write directly to him, but I think you are old enough to take care of it. Besides, here is a letter in a sealed envelope for you to tuck into the box when the roses come. It is for Mother, and no one else."

What fun to share a surprise with Father! E. McBean had a greenhouse and tiny shop at the edge of town. Eben hurried out there after school the next day.

The florist looked at Father's check. "Yellow! Hm-m!" he murmured. "Most expensive roses to be had. Will cost fifty cents more than this." He waved the check.

Eben never thought of telling the florist that Father might soon come home, and would then pay the balance. "I'll be back," he said, and dashed out of the shop. He ran lickety-split to Mrs. Hill's house.

"Could you let me have the fifty cents you will owe me two weeks from now?" he panted. "I'll wash Trixy extra good and stay and romp with her even if my father is at home," he promised, recklessly. He had to tell Mrs. Hill that it had something secret to do with Mother's birthday, before she would advance the money.

Eben rushed back to the florist's shop. Mr. McBean looked at the fifty-cent piece, and then at Eben. "Where'd you get it, so quick?" he asked. Eben explained. He thought that Mr. McBean and Mrs. Hill might have trusted him, without so much talk.

November the twelfth arrived. Yet Father had

not come. The house was bright and garnished. A wood fire burned on the hearth. Father's big chair, deep and soft, sat there, waiting. The *Cow and Hen Journal* was at its right hand, smoothed out, ready to tell Father the latest news about cows and hens. Father's roses, that Eben had secretly helped to buy, were on the piano. Father's letter, that no one could read but Mother, was tucked in her belt. The beautiful frosted cake that Granzie had made and decked with candles was in the center of the dining-table. The candle-light blurred and shimmered when one's eyes grew teary because Father was not there.

Still, there is no song more gay than "Happy Birthday to You." Granzie and Eben and Jerry sang it to Mother almost as bravely as if Father were there, while Joe banged the tray of his high chair with a spoon.

It seemed the dead of night when Eben awakened with an uneasy feeling. Perhaps it was too much rich frosting. Perhaps it was the ache that had gone to bed with him because Father had not come. No, it was something Eben had forgotten. He sat up in bed and rumpled his already rumpled hair, trying to remember.

"Hey, is that it?" Eben reached across to the other bed and gave his brother a punch. "You asleep, Jerry?" he whispered.

"Un-n-g," grunted Jerry.

"Wake up," urged Eben. "Maybe I forgot to close the gate to the cow lot when I brought Pansy in from pasture. Come on! We've got to find out."

Jerry rolled over, like one of his caterpillars in its cocoon. He slid deeper under the blankets.

Eben made a face at Jerry in the darkness. No good trying to wake him. Eben sat there, his arms folded over his knees. Perhaps he was worrying all for nothing. And who could expect a boy, a skinny boy only nine-and-a-half years old, to go scouting around by himself through the dark night after a silly cow? But what if Pansy had really strayed away! "Take good care of Mother and Granzie and Jerry and Joe, and of Pansy." That's what Father had said.

Eben felt his way to the window overlooking the back yard and the cow lot. He shivered. How dark it was! From the street-lamp in front of Mr. Sawyer's house there came only the faintest spread of light.

Fumbling for his clothes, Eben pulled them on. Shoes in hand, he tiptoed toward the door. That scamp Jerry! An old broom-handle with which Jerry had been playing, rolled under Eben's foot. When he threw out his hands to balance himself, he banged his knuckles against the dresser. To Eben it sounded like a pistol shot. Mother would be frightened. Granzie would think that robbers were in the house. Eben waited, scarcely breathing.

He picked up the broom-handle. It would be a good weapon in case he met any monsters. He crept down the back stairs, stopping now and then to listen. He had a strange feeling of being almost afraid of himself. Softly he shot the bolt of the kitchen door. Lightly as a cat he crossed the back porch and stepped out on the grass.

How dark! How still! There were few stars in the sky. That shadow at the corner of the house—did it move? Eben's heart thumped like a drum as he stole through the yard. It seemed to sink to his toes when he saw the darker square of the cow-shed door. It was open.

He switched on the light, just for an instant. Pansy was not in her stall. Neither was she in the lot. The outer gate was wide open. Pansy—Father's expensive hobby—where was she?

Eben looked at the house with longing. Surely

he was the only person awake in Sidneyville. He would go back and slip into his warm bed. At the first glimmer of dawn, he would get up and make a search for Pansy. But how a fellow could sleep these dark November mornings! Granzie and Mother were always up first.

Mr. Sawyer! There was a neighbor who was always willing to help. Eben took a step forward. He stopped. Mr. Sawyer's house was dark. Of course he was sound asleep. And somehow Eben didn't want Mr. Sawyer to know that he had been so careless as to leave the gate open, any more than he wanted Mother and Granzie to know it.

If only he could go to the Bradley house and call Peaches to his aid with a rattle of gravel thrown against the window, as the hero sometimes did, in books! But where was any gravel to be had? "Anyway," thought Eben, "the gravel would prob'ly wake up Peaches' mother, and not Peaches."

[159]

Eben sighed, and straightened his shoulders. He must set forth alone. First he would look along the railroad tracks. Last year there had been an item in the county paper that told of a cow being killed by a train, not far from Sidneyville. The ten-forty express that roared through the village without stopping, had it gone through yet? There was the one o'clock bus from Edenburn, too. Pansy might even cause a bad wreck. It was easy to imagine dreadful things in the silence of the night.

Toward the edge of town Eben crept like a ghost. His head turned owl-like at every imagined noise, at every shadow. Reaching the tracks, he knew by the light that burned in the station window half a mile away, that the night operator was still on duty. The ten-forty had not come through, then. Eben peered in the opposite direction. His heart jumped. What was that dark bulk at the side of the tracks?

[160]

Fearfully he crept forward. The black shadow moved. Surely it was too big for a mere cow. Eben stopped, backed up, and stared. But now he could see the faint shine of the brass tips on the animal's horns. Pooh, it must be—bravely Eben advanced. Yes, it was Pansy the Third, grazing on the sparse winter grass along the tracks.

Suddenly Eben heard the ten-forty screaming beyond the bend. At the very same moment Pansy stepped full upon the tracks. Eben plunged forward, brandishing the broom-handle. "Hi, Pansy! Hi!" Pansy did not budge. Eben could see the gleam of the approaching headlights reflected in her eyes. He could hear the train roaring down upon them, the warning whistle. There were precious lives on that train. Soldiers, perhaps. And in the path of the flyer—Pansy. The fine, pedigreed cow so dear to Father!

With frantic, frog-like leaps, Eben reached the

[161]

cow. Lifting the broom-handle, he gave her a terrific whack. Then he was cowering halfway down
the embankment, shielding his eyes from the
shower of gravel and cinders as the train flashed by.

When its roar had sunk to a far humming, Eben
scrambled to the tracks again. They were empty.
Where was Pansy? Had she been killed? At least
she had not wrecked the train. He heard thudding
footfalls. Peering through the faint starlight, he
saw the Jersey running along the opposite ditch.
Now, when it was almost too late, Pansy was frightened!

It took Eben several moments to catch her. She
was easily soothed. Soon they were walking homeward. Eben's knees were still shaking. But somehow he was no longer afraid. Not a bit afraid!

There was a light in the house when he locked
the gate and turned Pansy into her stable. His
mother stood anxiously at the kitchen door. She

[162]

With frantic leaps Eben reached the cow.

had wakened to feel that something was wrong, and to find that Eben was not in his bed. She was about to call Mr. Sawyer, she said. But when Eben told her, with boyish briefness, of the night's events, she looked at him with shining eyes. She stirred the fire. She seated Eben in Father's big chair. Smiling, she served him hot milk-and-bread in Father's big, gilt-edged coffee cup.

"For the young man-of-the-house," said Mother.

"Cripes," said Eben, though his heart leaped to hear Mother call him that. "A man-of-the-house wouldn't have left the gate open in the first place."

"No, he wouldn't," agreed Mother. "But to correct your mistake in the dark, in the cold— that took true courage." Mother smiled. "By-the-way, Eben," she whispered, "take notice that you did it without your father's necktie!"

Eben's mouth fell open. So he had! Why, so he had! He hung his head, grinning. That necktie business—all of a sudden it seemed as if it had been believed in by a boy he used to know. A kid who didn't know any better. Jiminy, now he knew that of course it isn't a dad's necktie that counts. It's what a dad *is*, himself, and a dad's trust in his son.

When Eben and Mother went upstairs, there was Granzie in the hall. She had to hear the story. "Of course you should not have gone out alone," she scolded. "Something dreadful might have happened to you." She turned to Mother. With her head up, she said, "I've always said that Eben is like my side of the family. It beats all how he resembles his great-grandfather Ebenezer. Ebenezer —*stone of help*," added Granzie, softly.

XIII

Captain Tuttle Comes Home

WHEW, but he was sleepy! Eben stretched and yawned and shivered and yawned again. He wished he didn't have to get up this morning. He opened one eye, and squinted at Jerry.

Jerry was wide awake. He was sitting up in bed, staring at the door. Someone laughed. A deep, hearty voice. A man's voice, laughing. Eben and Jerry threw off their bedclothes. They sprang out of bed. They raced across the room and fell into strong, outstretched arms.

"Father! Daddy! Father!" they screamed.

"Jerry! Eben! My big boys!" Father lifted them off their feet, hugging them.

"When did you come, Father?" they gasped.

[167]

"I came through Sidneyville last night on that ten-forty express Pansy tried to wreck!" chuckled Father. "You had no more than gone to bed yourself, Eben, when I arrived on the one o'clock bus from Edenburn. Mother and Granzie and I sat up almost all night, talking. There was so much to say. I've heard of everything that's happened in this house since I left home. For instance, I've heard that Jerry has been a very good boy, as I asked him to be."

Jerry blushed and tried to hide behind Father. But his mouth turned up at the corners.

"I heard a lot of stories," said Father. "Stories about smashed strawberry pies and green paint and neckties." He paused, while Eben wished he could crawl under the bed. "And I heard stories about war stamps and Red Cross Fairs," continued Father, "and Aunt May's dog. I even heard a story from McBean the florist, who hap-

[168]

pened to be on the bus last night. It was a story about some yellow roses, and a boy who paid the extra money for them, and never bragged about it, nor even said a word about it to anyone." Father laid his hand on Eben's head. "Thanks, pal, for helping me out."

Suddenly Father picked up a pillow and flung it in Eben's face. He snatched up another one and crammed it down on Jerry's shoulders. The fight was on—a glorious fight. Like the ones they used to have, only better.

They were red and tumbled and breathless when a voice came soaring up. "A wonderful breakfast will grow cold if you don't hurry down," called Mother. So they had a race. Who would get dressed first? Jerry won, and clattered downstairs, though Eben shouted after him that he hadn't laced his shoes.

Eben and Father walked down the steps, hand-in-hand. "After breakfast we'll go out and say 'hello' to Pansy the Third," said Father. "And by-the-way, that was a real story! It happened only last night. A story of pluck."

"Oh, *that!*" said Eben. "I was scared, Father. I was the scaredest I've ever been in my whole life!"

But by this time they were in the dining room. Everyone sat down to the table. "My!" exclaimed Granzie, drawing a deep, happy breath. "It is good to have the man-of-the-house at home again!"

Father's eyes traveled quickly around the table. He laughed, lifted his glass of tomato juice that Mrs. Sawyer had sent over with her compliments. "Here's to Uncle Sam," said Father, "who allowed me to come home to the Tuttles. Here's to Mrs. John Tuttle, who has no equal. Here's to Granzie, the best of grandmothers. Here's to Joey, whose smiles never come off. Here's to Jerry, a very good boy." Father paused for a moment, while Eben held his breath. What would Father say about him?

"And here's to Eben," said Father, "our young man-of-the-house!"

THE END